or fore   D0833599

DOGS
AND PUPPIES

ROSE HILL

Shetland
Sheepdog

Watch the dog run

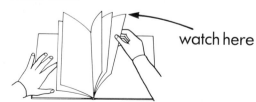

Hold the
book like
this.

Watch the top right hand
corner and flick the pages
over fast.

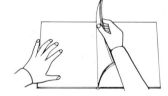

watch here

Being a dog owner

A dog will become a member of your family. There are some important things for you and your parents to think about before your family gets a dog. You will need your parents' help to look after it and train it.

Dogs live for about 14 years. A dog needs looking after every day of its life. You will have to feed it, take it for walks, play with it and groom it.

This dog is waiting to go for its evening walk.

This dog has been left alone for too long. It is making a noise because it is unhappy. Your neighbours may complain.

Dogs like company so much that they must not be left alone for more than a few hours.

Take your dog for its walks at about the same time every day.

Irish Setter

Owning a dog costs money. You will need money to buy the dog, to buy a collar, lead and basket. You will have to buy food and pay for vet's bills, and for kennels when you go away on holiday.

Bearded Collie

Your parents may need to put up a strong high fence round the garden, to stop the dog escaping.

German Shepherd Dog

Dog owners have laws to obey. You must buy a name and address tag and a licence for your dog. In some countries, your dog must wear a licence tag on its collar, and a tag to say that it has been vaccinated against rabies.

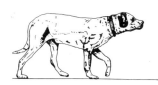

You must keep your dog on a lead on the roads, and in most public places.

If your dog is loose and runs into the road, it may cause an accident. This can cost the dog owner a lot of money.

A dog needs a lot of looking after and training. But with care and affection it will become a loyal friend, ready to join in with your games.

Sheep are frightened of dogs, and can even be killed by them. A farmer may shoot a dog if it is a nuisance. You may be fined if your dog chases farm animals.
You may also be fined if your dog fouls footpaths and you can get into trouble if your dog bites someone.

3

Choosing a dog

These pages will help you choose what kind of dog you want. There are about 200 breeds of dog. You can see some of them in this book. Read other books about them, and talk to dog owners you know.

Big dogs are very strong. They need a lot of space in the house and garden, and a big open space nearby for walks. They need a lot of food as well as exercise.

Afghan Hound

Yorkshire Terrier

Small dogs need less food and space, but they can be quite fierce.

This dog's coat needs clipping – it can't see!

Long-haired dogs need a lot of regular grooming.

Old English Sheepdog

A big dog can knock you down even when it is being friendly.

Some dogs are bred for their looks rather than for the way they behave. So you should find out as much as possible about your favourite breed. Ask your local vet for advice, and talk to local breeders.

A mongrel is a mixture of breeds. Mongrels are often very good-natured, and they are cheaper to buy than pedigree dogs.

You won't know how big a mongrel puppy will grow, even if you see the mother.

This little puppy...

grew to this size!

Choosing a puppy

Once you have decided what kind of dog you would like, find a breeder or a private home where puppies are for sale, or ask at an animal welfare organization. If the puppies are pedigreed, ask your local vet for advice on the breed.

The owner should let you see the puppies with their mother. Choose a healthy puppy that is friendly, alert, playful and interested in you. It mustn't be too fat or too thin. It should have bright eyes, and a clean coat, ears and nose.

Jack Russell

5

Your puppy's new home

Before you bring your puppy home, you will need quite a few things for it. It's nice to choose a name for the puppy so that you can start using its name as soon as you bring it home.

West Highland White Terrier

Safe toys to play with.

When you collect the puppy, you should take a strong box with you, lined with newspaper. The puppy will never have been on a lead, and it will be safer and happier tucked up in a box.

At first everything will seem strange and frightening for your puppy. Welcome it with some food and water and stroke it gently. Don't give it too many new people to meet.

Your dog must have its own bed. Give your puppy a box rather than an expensive bed, as the puppy may tear or chew it up. The bed must be away from draughts and damp. (You can raise it off the floor on piles of magazines.)

The bed must be big enough for the dog to curl up in comfortably.

Line the bed with a washable blanket on top of newspaper.

Cocker Spaniel

Leave plenty of newspaper around the bed.

Puppies may cry on their first few nights with you, because they miss sleeping with their brothers, sisters and mother. Don't go to your puppy every time it cries. If you do, it will cry whenever you leave it.

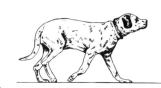

You could give your puppy a warm hot water bottle wrapped in a cloth, and a ticking clock for company.

Bassett Hound

Beagle

Your puppy will soon stop being afraid. It will rush around exploring and licking everything it can – including you!

Puppy collars

Your puppy will need a puppy collar and lead. The collar should be loose enough for two fingers to fit inside, when the puppy is wearing it.
As your dog grows, it will need a bigger and stronger collar and lead.

elastic

Puppy collar.

Disc with your address on.

Contact your local vet at once. Your puppy may need worming and vaccinations against illnesses before it is 3 months old.

Handling a puppy

When you pick up a puppy, always use both hands. Do not pick it up under its stomach or by its front legs.

One hand supports the front legs.

The other supports the back legs.

Hold it firmly, but not tightly, to stop it jumping down. Never try to pick up a big dog.

7

Feeding dogs and puppies

In the wild, dogs have to search or hunt for food, so they eat as much as possible when they find food. Pet dogs will do the same, but it is not kind to let your dog eat too much at once, or to leave it for too long without feeding.

Feeding puppies

Young puppies need 4 meals a day at first, since their stomachs are quite small. You can feed yours on mixtures of canned, semi-moist, dried or fresh meat, biscuits, cereals and milk. You should always leave it fresh water. When your puppy is 3 months old, it can have 3 bigger meals a day. By 6 months it will only need 2 larger meals. Make the meals bigger by adding more meat and biscuits but less milk. By 9 months, most dogs do well on one meal a day.

Feeding adult dogs

Adult dogs do well on mixtures of meats, cereals and biscuits. Canned, semi-moist or dried food is easy to give, together with biscuits and water. The amount your dog needs depends on its size. You can get advice about this from vets or dog breeders. Feed your dog at the same time, and in the same place every day. Dogs need water at all times.

West Highland White Terrier

As puppies get older, they need bigger meals but less often.

When you feed your puppy **canned or dried foods,** it is best to use the ones made for puppies. When you feed your puppy **fresh foods,** it will need a mixture of meat, cereal and warm milk. The meat can be red or white meat and it should all be finely chopped. Cereals are things like porridge, brown bread or puppy meal. Ask your vet for advice about how to make up a balanced diet for your dog.

If you watch your dog eating, you will see that it doesn't chew its food. Adult dogs have big stomachs which can take large lumps of food. They need to rest after a meal in order to digest their food.

Great Dane

Tall dogs need their bowls raised off the floor.

Chocolate Labrador

Dogs love bones. Bones are good for their teeth and gums. But only give your dog big, raw marrow bones. Chicken bones and other small sharp bones are dangerous.

Bloodhound

Dogs with long ears need small bowls with steep sides.

Dogs are greedy. Don't feed your dog with titbits between meals or when you are eating. Too many sweet things are bad for your dog.

Black Labrador

Dogs may steal food even if they aren't hungry.

In the house

Sleeping

Pet dogs usually live indoors. Your dog must have a bed of its own. Once your dog is fully grown, you can buy it a new bed. There are many different kinds of bed for dogs. The one you choose must be big enough for the dog to turn round in, and easy enough to clean.

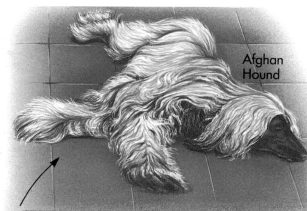

Cavalier King Charles Spaniel

Dogs sleep for about 14 hours each day. Puppies sleep for even longer.

Yellow Labrador

The bed is your dog's own place in the house. It may hide its favourite toys or bones there, and will go there when it wants to be by itself.

Afghan Hound

Guarding the house

Bulldog

Any breed which lives and sleeps indoors and which barks at sudden noises will help to guard the house.

Dogs often like sleeping on hard surfaces, especially when it is warm or sunny. They may stretch out to enjoy it.

Toilet training

At 8 weeks old, a puppy may make 12 puddles a day! But puppies soon learn not to make a mess in the house. Your puppy is most likely to want to go to the lavatory when it wakes up, and after each meal or drink. When it wants to go, it will probably sniff the floor and circle round. Put your puppy outside at these times, and praise it when it manages to go to the lavatory outside.

If you catch it making a puddle inside, say "No!" firmly. Don't shout or hit your puppy. It will know by the tone of your voice that it has done wrong. Clean up any mess properly. Wash your hands afterwards.

Put your puppy outside when it wants to go to the lavatory.

Be careful, especially when your dog is a puppy, not to leave small or sharp objects lying around – your puppy could swallow them. Plastic bags are also dangerous – your puppy could suffocate inside one. Protect electric flex – your puppy could bite through it to the live wire. Don't leave your toys and slippers around with the puppy if you don't want them chewed up!

Cairn Terrier

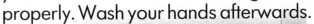

Cocker Spaniel

Another way of toilet training is to make the puppy go to the lavatory on newspaper. Start off with lots of sheets on the floor. Gradually take bits away until you have just one sheet by the door. Then move the sheet into the garden. Your puppy should then learn to ask to go out.

11

Playing

Dalmatian

Puppies love to play with anything. They learn things and get exercise from playing. But they do less damage if they have their own toys.

If you buy a ball, it must be the right size for your dog. It must be big enough not to get swallowed. Balls or other toys made of soft rubber are dangerous. The dog may chew them and swallow the rubber.

If you play with sticks, make sure they are not sharp or have nails sticking out. Never throw stones, as your dog may swallow them or hurt its teeth.

Some dogs like to play hide and seek. Make your dog sit while you hide a toy, and then let the dog look for the toy.

Some dogs enjoy swimming. You can throw sticks into the water for them to fetch.

Munsterlander

Many dogs enjoy fetching and bringing. If you throw a stick, they will fetch it, and bring it back to you. This is fun and good exercise for your dog.

12

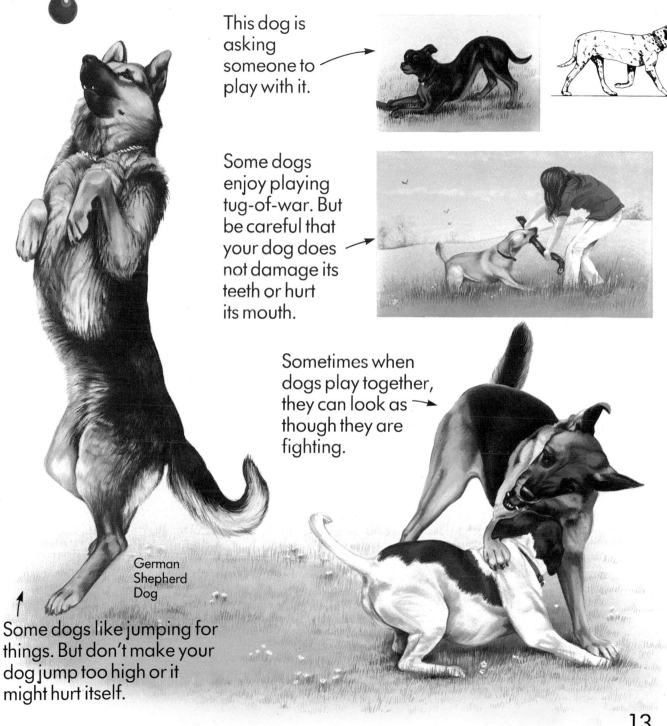

This dog is asking someone to play with it.

Some dogs enjoy playing tug-of-war. But be careful that your dog does not damage its teeth or hurt its mouth.

Sometimes when dogs play together, they can look as though they are fighting.

German Shepherd Dog

Some dogs like jumping for things. But don't make your dog jump too high or it might hurt itself.

13

Looking after your dog

Exercise

Adult dogs need to be taken for a walk outside. Start taking your dog out on the lead while it is still young. You must train it to come when you call before you can let it off the lead (see pages 16-17).

German Shepherd Dog

Dogs like to run freely and explore. They like to sniff different scents and meet other dogs. A short walk and run off the lead in a safe place is much better than a long walk on the lead.

English Setter

Puppies get all the exercise they need from playing at home and in the garden. They shouldn't be allowed beyond the garden until they have been vaccinated.

Collars and leads

You will need to choose the right collar and lead for your dog. The pet store assistant should be able to help you.

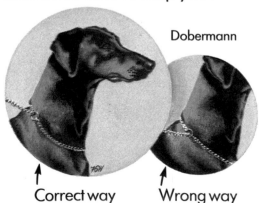

Dobermann

Correct way   Wrong way

Sometimes a choke chain lead (see pictures) is used as a training aid. This type of lead can hurt a dog and must be used carefully. A choke chain should not normally be used in place of an ordinary collar and lead.

Bassett Hound

A male dog will mark out its trail on a walk by urinating on things it passes such as lampposts or trees. By doing this it leaves its scent. It will also sniff the trails of other dogs who have left their scents. Each dog has its own scent.

Grooming

You should brush or comb your dog's coat regularly to keep it clean and healthy.

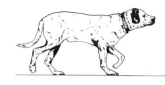

Short-haired dogs only need brushing. You can use an old soft hairbrush.

Long-haired dogs need combing as well as brushing, every day.

St Bernard

Washing

If your dog rubs itself in smelly things like cow pats you may have to give it a bath.

Miniature Poodle

You can bath a small dog in the sink, but large dogs will have to be done in the garden with a watering can or hose. Always use warm water and a special dog shampoo. Rinse it well. Dry it with its own towel, and keep it warm afterwards. You should dry your dog after a walk in the rain too.

Training your dog

The best way to train your dog is to let only one person (usually an adult) be in charge of the lessons. Do them in an enclosed garden, or a space that the dog knows. Start when your dog is about six months old.

Always use a firm kind voice, and say only short simple words. Always say the words in the same way, and your dog will learn to recognize them quickly. Give it lots of praise every time it does the correct thing. Be patient and never lose your temper with your dog.

Regular, short lessons are much better than one long lesson. Train your dog for 5-10 minutes at a time, two or more times a day.

There are four basic things your dog should learn.

HEEL

First it should learn to walk to heel. Once the puppy has got used to a collar, attach a lead, and let the puppy run around by itself. Then hold the lead so that the puppy is just behind your left leg, with its head close to your leg. Say "heel" and begin to walk. If it tries to overtake you, or pulls away, pull it back to you firmly and say "heel" again. Praise it when it begins to walk in the correct position.

SIT

Then it should learn to sit. Let your dog stand still, then say "sit" and at the same time push down firmly on its behind, until it is forced into the sitting position. Praise it. Repeat this until the dog doesn't need you to press down at all, and sits just at your command.

Don't push down too hard. You might hurt the dog.

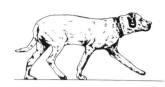

Labrador

If your dog is well-trained, both of you will be able to enjoy yourselves more. You will be able to do more together because you know your dog will obey your commands at a time when it may be dangerous.

STAY

Sometimes you will want your dog to stay in the same sitting position. Once it has learned to sit, say "stay" and take a few steps backwards. Your dog will try to follow you. Say "stay" again and make it sit. Keep praising it when it stays sitting, and gradually it will learn to stay.

COME

Lastly, you must be able to call your dog to you. This is an important lesson. By now your dog should know its name. Attach a long piece of string to the lead, and make your dog sit. Then say "stay" and walk backwards a few steps. Then say "come" and call the dog's name. At the same time, pull gently but firmly on the string. Praise the dog when it comes to you. Gradually walk farther backwards until you have let all the string out. After a few lessons you should be able to call the dog to you without using the lead.

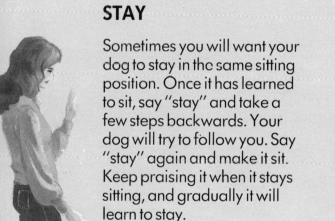

Golden Retriever

Travelling

Most dogs love car journeys. But sometimes puppies are travel sick on their first few journeys, so it's best to keep these short. Some dogs become restless on journeys. Your dog must learn to sit still.

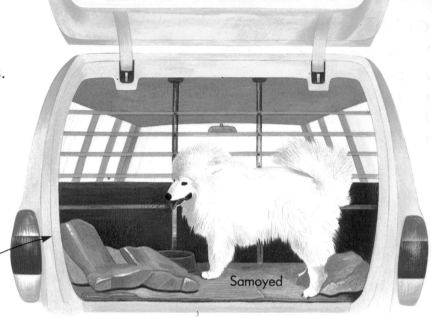

Samoyed

Some cars have room to keep your dog at the back behind a wire guard.

On long journeys, take fresh water and your dog's bowl so that you can give it a drink when it gets thirsty. If you are driving, stop now and then and let your dog out on its lead.

You should not allow your dog to hang its head out of the window when the car is moving. This is dangerous for the dog, and may hurt its eyes.

English Springer Spaniel

You musn't leave a puppy alone inside a parked car, even for a few minutes. Don't leave an adult dog alone in the car if you can avoid it. If you do it will become very unhappy. If you must leave your dog in the car, make sure the car is parked in the shade. Never leave a dog in the car if it is very hot or very cold.

You should have at least two windows wide enough open to let fresh air in, but not so wide that the dog can get out through them.

On holiday

When you take your dog on holiday, it may take a while to settle in. A country dog may be frightened by town traffic and noises. A town dog may get very excited in the country and might start chasing farm animals. Always keep your dog on a lead at first. To help your dog settle in, take along its bed and feeding bowls.

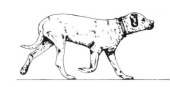

Golden Retriever

Some dogs enjoy swimming and playing in water. Call your dog back before it swims off too far, or annoys other people. Don't let your dog swim in rivers with a strong current.

At the beach, you should bring fresh water and your dog's bowl. If it drinks sea water, it may be sick. Never let your dog go to the lavatory on the beach.

Boarding kennels

If it's impossible for your dog to come with you on holiday, and if there is no one to look after it, you could take the dog to boarding kennels. You will need to book a place for the dog before you go away, and you will have to show its vaccination certificate.

If you move house, your dog might be happier in kennels while you are moving.

Most dogs are happy in kennels once their owners are out of sight.

19

Your dog's health

If your dog suddenly starts behaving in a strange way, it may be ill. Dogs will often vomit (be sick). Sometimes they eat grass to help themselves vomit. But if your dog doesn't want to eat for more than two days, or keeps on vomiting or having diarrhoea, it may be seriously ill. You should take it to the vet.

Cavalier King Charles Spaniel

Worms

If your dog seems to be much more hungry than usual, and yet it seems to be getting thinner, it may have worms. All dogs, especially puppies, need medicine for worms regularly. Your vet will give you some worm pills.

Scratching

If your dog scratches a lot, or bites its skin, it's probably trying to get rid of an itch. You should take it to the vet. He may say that grooming will help. Or your dog may have fleas. The vet will give you some flea spray or powder. If your dog shakes its head a lot, or scratches around the ears, you should take it to the vet. Ears are very delicate.

Chow Chow

Dogs often cut their paws. Always clean up cuts, and bandage them if necessary. If your dog gets a bad wound, you should take it to the vet.

Rabies is a disease which kills people. It can be caught from dogs with the disease if they bite you. In countries where rabies is found, dogs must be vaccinated against it. In other countries, such as Britain, where rabies isn't found, it is against the law to bring dogs in from abroad unless they go into quarantine.

Mating

A female dog is called a bitch. She can have puppies from the age of about six months. Twice a year she will be "in season" and will be ready to mate with a male dog and have puppies. You can tell when your bitch is coming into season. You will see spots of blood around her hindquarters. She will become very attractive to male dogs.

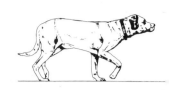

Male dogs can smell these changes in female dogs. They may come and sniff her. If you don't want your bitch to have puppies, you must guard her closely when she is in season. Keep her on the lead when you take her out.

Foxhound

Male dogs may try to run away to mate with your dog. Sometimes they wait outside a bitch's house for days. Keep your bitch indoors when she is in season.

But the best thing to do if you don't want your bitch to have puppies is to have her neutered. Your vet can do this by a simple operation when she is five months old. This is kinder than having unwanted puppies destroyed.

Having puppies

If you do want your dog to have puppies, and you know that they will go to good homes, you should find a mate of the same breed for her. You must give your dog extra care for 9 weeks after the mating, and for a month or two after the birth. When your dog is pregnant, take it to the vet for a check up.

West Highland White Terrier

After your bitch has mated, puppies may start to form inside her. This is called being "pregnant". You will notice her tummy and nipples begin to swell. She will become less playful. She must be given plenty of milk, less cereal and more meat. Start giving her extra food 3 weeks before the puppies are due.

Two weeks before her puppies are due (about 7 weeks after mating) line your dog's bed with newspaper. She may tear it up to make a nest. Just before she gives birth, your bitch will seem restless. She will go to her nest. She needs to be left in peace, but with someone nearby.

A puppy is born in a sac, which the mother chews open to free the puppy, before the next one is born. The mother licks each puppy clean. There may be as many as 10 puppies if your dog is large. A smaller dog has 4-6 puppies.

Dachshund

22

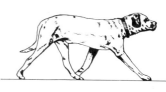

Puppies are blind and deaf when they are born. They begin to see and hear at about 8 days old. They cannot walk, but use their front legs to drag themselves along.

The mother will need extra food while the puppies are feeding on her milk. By the time the pups are 3 weeks old, she may need 3 times as much as usual.

Rough Collie

You should try not to touch the puppies for about two weeks after they are born. You may upset their mother. She may try to protect them, even from people she knows.

At 3 weeks old, the puppies can walk. They will leave the nest and begin to explore. At this time you should start to feed the puppies small meals. You can buy special puppy food.

A puppy will probably walk into a saucer of food before it learns to eat from it.

Beagle

Picture puzzle

There are 13 dogs hidden in this picture.
Can you find them all?